Rose in the Wind

Rose in the Wind

Paperback ISBN: 979-8-9860947-5-5

Editor: Crystal S. Wright

10 9 8 7 6 5 4 3 2 1

Printed in the United States

Priceless Publishing®
pricelesspublishing.co
Lauderhill, Florida

Contents

The wind blew a
rose my way

Karrington Danielle Rose:

A ROSE IN THE WIND

Karrington Danielle Rose has been flirting with Dominique McCullin in her head for a very long time, but his cavalier demeanor and arrogance have always made her nervous.

Shit, I don't even think I can ask him what time it is. How could I ask him if he'd like to have a drink with me? He leaves at 5 on the dot every day, so maybe I could just conveniently be on my way out too. Karrington was busy thinking through a strategy.

Karrington is the middle child of three and she's also a *daddy's girl*. Karrington and her mom are extremely close as well — her mom was the only person she confided in about her divorce and other hardships she faced. Her sister, Kelsey, lives in Atlanta with her family and her brother, Karson, is in Seattle with his family.

After going through a horrific divorce, herself, she felt she needed a fresh start and since she was more flexible than her siblings, she felt the need to be closer to home since their parents are getting older. After searching for months, she came across the Fairfax District Attorney's office, put in her resume and the rest is history!

Karrington is a very confident woman who has always gone for what she wants. Her 5'7" frame was small and shapely. Her hair has been a dark red all of her life and with the

newfound freedom she has, she decided to go darker brown which coats her caramel skin and makes her a standout among her peers. Since she's been in her new position, nothing has changed. She still stands out among the other females in the office.

Not that she thought Dominique should have said something by now, but she felt like at least they should have met. It was just something about Dominique that stifled her a bit, but she gave herself a pep talk like always and put her plan in motion. *Karri, he puts his pants on one leg at a time...get him.* That always made her laugh to herself, but this one required a little more finesse, cause he was 'the man' around the office and she didn't want to be *that girl.*

Dominique McCullin is the most eligible bachelor in Fairmont, and he knows it too. He would swagger into a courtroom with his 6'3" frame, and his no nonsense persona and even cause judges to be intimated. His cases were legendary and this made him one of the most feared attorneys in the northern tri state area.

Dominique has worked his way up with his wins and is very much respected by his peers. He has recruited the top formidable group of attorneys in West Virginia who are almost as untouchable as he is. For this reason, this DA's office stands above the rest.

On this particular Friday, before Karrington was going to put her plan in place, she got a surprise that she was not prepared for. Dominique walked past her door and a deep voice fired off three statements.

"Hello. So, you are the new kid on the block? Karrington, right?"

As Karrington turned in her seat she saw that his height and brown skin fit perfectly with the navy suit he was wearing. He looked regal.

She managed to get her tongue to work and said, *"Hello, Mr. McCullin. It is so nice to finally meet you. I was feeling a little like an outcast after being here for a week, Sir."*

Karrington is a flirt at heart, but she knows how to turn it up or tone it down. In this moment, she was very toned down. Dominique went on to let her know that he had every intention to stop by to meet her sooner, but had been tackling a very high-profile case. But he promised to make it his priority to welcome her properly to the office before he left for the day.

Dominique usually leaves the office at five o'clock sharp every day, but today he sat and talked to Karrington. He likes to know about all his employees to get a feel of where they would be the most successful in the office, since they have to work so close and depend on each other.

"So Karrington, where are you from?" he asked.

Karrington faced her new and attractive coworker and said as professionally as she could, *"I am from Morgantown, not far from here. My parents are still there. Fairmont is just far away enough that I can check on them and still have a life."*

Dominique laughed and continued to inquire about Karrington, realizing that she is an incredible attorney who built up a stack of wins at her previous office in Missouri. He was extremely impressed with her and said, *"Next week I may want you to look over this case I was telling you about. You are someone who should be on this team."*

Karrington was beaming and although all she wanted to do was kiss him, the invitation to work closely with him on a big case was an even bigger prize. Being super competitive, she decided to hold off on pursuing the drink and kiss, and focus on what she loves the most...the win!

"Mr. McCullin, thank you so much. I will be looking forward to Monday!" she exclaimed.

Dominique, in his next breath said, *"Call me Dom — we are about to really get to know each other. When we have cases like this my nights are long, so yours will be too."*

Karrington smiled and her light brown eyes lit up as she said, *"I can't wait!"*

Dominique bid her good night and as he was leaving, she got up to leave as well. When he turned around and saw her preparing her things, he couldn't help but stare.

"Is there something wrong, Dom?"

Dominique stood there and as she walked closer to him, he could see that Karrington was not only astounding on paper, but studying her up close he noticed for the first time that she was breathtaking.

"No, nothing is wrong. Everything is just right."

Karrington tried to conceal her blush. Handbag in hand, she walked from her desk. They exited her office together and Dominique waited for her to lock her door. *"I've got to get out of here, I'm late for my Friday cigar! Talking with you, time passed so quickly."*

Karrington smirked and replied, *"That is one of my favorite things to do too."*

As she walked away, she couldn't help but think about her favorite Tupac song as she put a little twist in her hips while Dom stared.

On her drive home, Karrington could only think about the last hour of her day: the plan she had made to run into Dominique and the fortuitous visit she received without looking desperate. So, there was only one thing to do — call her girl, Gabby.

Karrington couldn't help but to think to herself how great they would be together. In the same moment she also thought about her failed relationships and that's usually how they started.

I need to refocus. I could really be reaching right now. If something is there, it will reveal itself. I just need to focus on Monday, but it's going to be hard because he is a lot to focus on..."

She nipped that mental tangent in the bud, picked up the phone and called Gabby. *"Hello,"* Gabby answered, Noting Karrington's hesitation she continued, *"What's going on now girl…talk to me. How is the new job going?"*

"Giiiiiirl," when Karrington says that, Gabby knows it's about to be good. *"So, there is this guy at my office. He is like the number one guy here so it's a little intimidating, but you know that won't phase me. I'll just have to be careful with this one."*

Gabby is just listening before she weighs in and Karrington knows it's coming, she's just waiting. *"Girl, what do you have to say,"* Karrington prompted.

Gabby cleared her voice and said, *"Friend, please take this slow. You go so deep so fast, that you just open yourself up to hurt and pain."* Gabby had been with Karrington through some of the worst times in her life, and Karrington knew exactly what her friend was talking about.

"I know, girl. I am going to take this slow. Hell, there may not be anything to speed up or slow down — he may not even see me like that. I'll call you later girl. I'm going to go and relax cause this has been a long week."

The two friends hung up as Karrington pulled into her condo with a night of relaxation on her mind.

In a garden of roses
I found you

Dominique McCullin:
A ROSE IN THE WIND

Dominique E. McCullin is the top attorney in the northern West Virginia tri-state area. He graduated at the top of his class in law school and is the oldest of four children who are just as successful as he. Dominique has had some revelations in his life and is now in a place of self-awareness, where he is clear on, and has accepted who he is.

Dominique is an alpha male who appreciates and respects women in his life. He is focused on his work as an attorney, but he wants a special woman who will understand and accept the man that he is. Dominique has a dark side that he keeps disciplined within himself until he encounters someone with whom he can completely share his lifestyle. He is patient in waiting for her.

As Dominique walked to his car, he realized that he was late meeting his frat brothers for their Friday brotherhood smoke. He couldn't help but to think this tardiness is justified and the frat can wait. *Karrington is justification enough*, he rationalized. Try as he might, he couldn't get her out of his mind.

Dominique believes that it's never good to have an office relationship. As a matter of fact, it is a part of the code of conduct in the office handbook. But as he continued to think about Ms. Rose, he couldn't help but chuckle to himself. *Some rules are made to be broken,* he thought.

As he pulled into the Cigar Lounge, he knew that being late meant that he had to buy the first two rounds, but after today, he'd buy rounds for the entire bar. *Karrington is worth it,* he thought. *She could be that special one.*

When Dominique walks into his section, it is smoky and filled with his friends. Colin spotted him immediately and chanted, *"Drinks on Dom...drinks on Dom!"*

Dom and his frat brothers all went to Bowie State and that's where their brotherhood began exactly a decade earlier. *"Man, I wasn't trying to be late, but I'm happy to buy these drinks."*

Colin and Dominique are the closest of the eight men. If anyone knows Dom, it's Colin and if anyone knows Colin, it's Dom. When Dom's face lit up about buying drinks, Colin looked over at him and said, *"Tell me about her later, Frat."*

Dominique smiled and replied, *"No doubt."*

Dom and his frat brothers had a great night of decompressing, catching up and making plans for upcoming events. As the night was coming to a close, Colin and Dom discussed their meetup time for basketball the next day.

On the way out, Dom said, *"Man, I think I found the one today. I don't know for sure, but I hope so!"*

Colin looked at Dominique because he's only heard that statement once before since he has known him, and that relationship almost took Dominique out.

Colin said, *"Man, are you sure? I know how serious you can get. I'm here for you, Frat, you know that."* With that they parted until morning.

Dominique drove home thinking about Karrington — who she could be to him and who he could be to her. Then he chided himself, *I may be jumping the gun, I may not be her type.*

Karrington AND Dominique

Karrington had the time of her life last night with Gabby and she was feeling it when she woke up. She was trying to decide if she was going to continue to lie in bed, or get up and go to the gym as she usually does on Saturday mornings. The gym won.

As she was preparing to go out, she couldn't help but to think of her interactions with Dominique after work on Friday.

I wonder how this is going to work. I may be jumping ahead of myself, but I really think he could be the one, she said to herself. *I feel like he could be into me, but he is so hard to read and has such a smart-ass mouth...ugh.*

Karrington, feeling like she may be getting ahead of herself yet again, resolved in her mind to do what she moved back East to do — continue to have a great law career and work on herself.

She grabbed her water bottle and keys and thought about her fitness goals. *Whatever happens, let me keep this frame tight just in case Mr. McCullin decides this is where he wants to be.* She laughed to herself, grabbed her headset and headed out.

Karrington calls her mother on her way to the gym and tells her she will be home tomorrow to go to church. *"Baby, I will be so happy to see you, but you're leaving in the morning? Why not tonight?"*

Karrington really wanted to relax and do some work at home, but her mom had a point, *"Mama, I'll do that. When I leave the gym, I'll go home and get some things together."*

Mrs. Rose told her she was going to cook for her after church and she was so happy. *"Ma, where is daddy?"*

It was impossible to miss the excitement in Karrington's voice.

Her mother answered, *"He's out in the garage tearing something up baby you know how your daddy is."*

Karrington told her she had made it to the gym and she'd give her a call when she got on the road. They said their goodbyes and hung up. As Karrington pulled into her gym parking lot, she couldn't believe her eyes. She saw the unforgettable physique of Dominique walking into her gym!

Karrington froze in her car seat and immediately felt that she should have probably stayed in bed, but she looked at this as another opportunity, especially since the gym is neutral ground.

I am so glad I wore my cute gym outfit, Karrington mouthed to herself as she readjusted her messy bun. *I cannot walk in here looking for him. I have to play this very cool. I'll sit here for another hot minute and then I will go in.*

Karrington had her game plan set but her heart was beating fast from anxiety and excitement! She grabbed her gym bag and got out of the car, turning to look at herself one last time in her car window. No ifs or buts about it — she is a beautiful woman, in and out. Her natural beauty is out of this world and she knows it. As she walks closer to the door, she catches a glimpse of Dominique.

Karrington tried to not appear too excited. *It's just another day in the gym,* she tells herself. *But today is a different day because Dominique is here!* Instead of starting with her usual stretching which would take her in the opposite direction, she chose to go in the direction of her Dark Knight. She secretly watched Dominique go into the men's locker room and positioned herself on the dreaded treadmill by the locker room.

Expecting him to light up her peripherals any minute, Karrington went into a light jog. Though nervous, but she was ready for this moment. As Dominique walks out of the locker room, Karrington looks up, feigning surprise, as if she had not been watching the door the entire time.

Dom's face lit up. *"Well, well, well, it's the new kid on the block in my gym!"* He walked over to the treadmill and checked the incline and speed, *"Looks like you are on your way."*

 She tried to appear as if she had been there for a while, but her time on the LED screen told on her.
"Look at you at my gym. This is such a surprise on a Saturday," she flirted back, hoping her anxiety was not noticeable.

They talked for a little while and they parted to continue their weekend workout. Dominique and his friends enjoyed their game and Karrington finished her workout.

After a while she couldn't see him and assumed he had left, so she prepared herself to leave. As she was walking out, she saw him standing next to her car. *"Did you have a good workout?"* he asked.

"Yes, I did. How was your game?" She asked, feeling her inner flirt awaken.

She and Dom continued to talk until he checked his watch and exclaimed, *"I don't know where the time goes with you but I should be home by now, Kid!"*

Smiling, Karrington said, *"Well, I have to get going too. I'm going to my parents' for church tomorrow. What are you doing?"*

Dom leaned down and said, *"After seeing you in the gym today, I was hoping to take you out before Monday. Is there any way I could do that?"*

Karrington smiled and said, *"Oh, really?* Pretending to think long and hard, she said, *"Well, I have to go to my parents today, but I will be back tomorrow morning before we have to be coworkers again. Will that work?"*

Dom nodded. *"All I need now is an address."* They exchanged numbers and went their separate ways.

Karrington rode home in silence with a smile. She was in fast forward mode having thoughts of her weekend plans. She could feel her heart beating — not the one in her chest — but the one that can get her into trouble. She thought about not going home, but she knew her parents were expecting her. She could not disappoint them.

As Dom was driving home, he was plagued with similar thoughts. He found himself excited and glad he was driving. He began to consider the kind of date that he wanted to take Karrington on. He felt like she was *the one,* so he knew exactly where he wanted to take her, but he didn't want to scare her off. Though he couldn't quite put his finger on it, there was something about Karrington that made her hard to resist. He couldn't wait to show her a great time.

Karrington made it home and prepared to travel to her parents. She was so glad that she had already told them that she'd be there from this evening and leaving right after church. Now she has more reason to get up and get her butt home early. *I don't even know what to pack with Dominique on my mind! I am so glad I am just 20 minutes away.*

She showered then hurriedly threw a church dress and something to drive back home in, in a bag and rushed out the door.

This drive is exactly what I need to decompress from the encounter at the gym today, she thought as she was on the highway. Thoughts of Dominique filled her mind on the highway so she began to talk things out.

I know this is a little meet up with Dominique, but I've been here for a minute and it's time. I can't be that girl! But then again, I can..." She bites her lip and laughs out loud while deftly maneuvering into the fast lane.

Karrington reaches her parent's home and is only too happy. Her dad was in the garage doing "dad stuff" when she pulled up.

"Hey, Daddy!" she screams.

He looks around quickly and says, *"Hi, Pudding!"*

She ran over to him and gave him a big hug and kiss. Fletcher Rose is a typical man's man. He's a retired military officer with a successful car dealership business that he chooses to check on when he's getting on his wife's nerves. He and Katherine had been married for 45 years and were happier than ever.

"Daddy, how have you been? I've missed you so much."

"Pudding, Daddy is getting along quite fine for an old man. Everything is good. How are you doing in the big city?"

She put her arms around him and gave him another kiss. *"It's going good. I love the work, the people, and my place. It's really good."*

They talked a little while longer before she headed into the house.

"Mommy!!!" she screamed.

Her mom turned around revealing a youthful face. You could tell that when she was Karrington's age, she was a very beautiful woman. Her hair is long and reddish blonde, her latte skin is slightly aged and her smile is amazing.

"Hey, baby. How are you? I'm so glad to see you! You want some coffee?"

She and her mom drank coffee together all the time. They got their cups and went into the living room to chat.

The thorn of a
rose can prick you

Dominique:

KARRINGTON'S THORN

Miles away in his apartment, Dominique was more than a little stressed. It was finally sinking in that he just asked his coworker out because he is thinking of her differently than he should.

Man, Karri is awesome and beautiful, but she is my coworker. I have to approach this carefully. What if she's not into what I'm into, how do I go about this?

Dominique headed to the shower. As he washed his chiseled chocolate frame, he was thinking about what he and Karrington could do tomorrow. *She said she liked cigars. Maybe I could take her to my special place...or we could just go to dinner.*

He kept going over the options in his head. Stepping out of the shower he skillfully wrapped a towel around his waist and walked toward his living room. He sat on the couch and grabbed the remote. He distractedly pressed the channel switch buttons but was really flipping through Sunday in his head.

I'm thinking about this too much, he reasons to himself. *It's just going to be dinner and conversation. She may not be the one or whatever.* But Dominque could not deny that Karrington awakened feelings in him that he had not felt in a really long time.

Dominique is all business when he's working and an extremely passionate man. He is very careful and intentional about the women he chooses to spend time with, which goes back to his ability to have so much restraint.

Dominique is the epitome of his name — he is a dominant alpha male who lives a dominating lifestyle. He always knew he was different than most when he was growing up. He would have girlfriends and he'd treat them like queens. He watched how his dad treated his mom, who was the happiest woman he knew. His father was a very smart and formidable provider who always put his family first. So, treating a woman well was in his DNA.

When he went to college, he thought something was wrong with him. He was told by women that he was too much or too aggressive. This bothered him, which is where the restraint came from, until one day he was approached by a girl who was friends with one of the girls he had dated.

She introduced him to the *lifestyle* and that day Dom realized that there was nothing wrong with him. He understood then that his desires and activity required a certain type of woman, and he was okay with that.

Thinking about Karrington made him feel his 'lifestyle' feelings and although he is one of the most confident men in West Virginia, he was nervous about his approach to her. Dominique had never been a man who wasted time, but his approach is respectful, but there is always a space for rejection.

It's only dinner but I need to at least text and give her some options," he said as he picked up his phone.

Karrington bid her mom good night and went to her room around 10pm, tired from the long day. She was ready for Sunday, but as she was getting into bed, she received a text. It was Dominique!

Kid, I'd like to thank you for accepting my date proposal. I can't wait to see you again. Dinner, a little dancing and I have a surprise for you to thank you for spending the night with me ;)

Karrington read the text over and over, butterflies in her stomach. *At least now I know a little bit about what the night will bring but what's that surprise about?* Soon she fell asleep deep in thought, forgetting to reply.

Sunday morning came. Karrington and her parents went to church together. She saw a lot of people that she had not seen in a while, and they were happy to see her. The elders reminisced about *'the Rose kids'*, who had been known to be very active in the community and church. Her parents beamed with pride with each compliment about Karrington or her siblings.

After church, Karrington ate with her parents and talked with them some more. They filled her in on all the personal updates that she had missed. She was so happy Fairmont was only 19 miles away, because she wanted to make the most of her Sunday afternoon.

Karrington didn't want to leave abruptly, so she continued to talk with them and then she looked at the clock. She knew she had a lot to do to prepare for her date so she started making her departure.

"Mommy, Daddy, I'm going to get ready to go. I want to get a little rest before my week starts. I'll be working on a new case so I need to relax a bit and get some stuff done at home."

Karrington kissed her parents' cheeks and walked to her car, thinking of Dominique and what the day would bring for them.

Being given a rose on a first date is every woman's dream

Karrington and Dominique:
DATE NIGHT

Sunday finally came and was set to be the most exciting day for Dominique and Karrington. She has gotten home from her parents', and called to let them know she made it home safely before collapsing on the couch.

I don't know what tonight is going to bring...but I know what I want it to bring.

She laughed to herself as she got off of the couch and started to do some house work. She walked from room to room thinking about what she wanted to wear and gradually became nervous.

I know this is a person who I work with, so I need to be careful. But, he is soooo fine! Karrington, just go with it and whatever the night brings, it brings.

She continued to coach herself as she finished up her chores. She couldn't help wondering what Dominique had in store for her.

Dom was mentally preparing for his date with Karri, and hoping she will be the one he's looking for. *I haven't felt like this about anyone in a very long time,* he admitted to himself.

He checked on dinner reservations for the night and prepared his car for the drive to The Riverside Club. *I'm just going with it. She seems to be excited and I'm certainly excited to see her again,* he said to himself.

He realized he had piqued Karrington's interest when he texted her on Saturday night asking for her email. He took his phone off of the charger to call her and check if she had made it from her parents', but his phone rang as soon as he reached for it. It was her.

Dominique answered and a smile slid across his face when he heard her voice, *"Hello, Kid,"* he said, *"You made it home?"*

"Yes, I did. I honestly can't wait to see you and find out what you have planned for me," she said.

Dominique took a breath and released words that surprised him, *"I have two requests: I would like for you to wear your sexiest little black dress and I would like for you to have an open mind. Is that too forward?"*

Karrington was quiet for a few seconds and a little fear came over Dominique. *Was that too forward? Had he scared her off? Was his tone offensive to her?*

Then she spoke, *"I think I can grant those. Your bold request actually takes the worry and wonder out of what to wear for you tonight, so no problem, Sir. I'm all yours..."* she said with happiness in her voice.

Dominique smiled and responded sweetly, *"We're already off to a good start. That's what I wanted to hear. I'm going to go and get dressed up for you and I will see you around 6:00."*

They got all of the particulars together and hung up. Dominique was very pleased, and started to get ready for the night.

Dominique is a well-dressed man any day of the week, but tonight was different — he wanted to impress someone... Karrington. He chose a black jacket with a white crisp button-down shirt and slacks that somehow made him look more attractive. *I really hope she likes how I look tonight. I know she will be beautiful.* He was right. Karrington is beautiful in her natural state, but when she gets ready to go out, she is breathtaking.

Karrington was as nervous as Dominique, or probably more so. Although she has what seems like 100 black dresses, none seemed good enough for Dominique. Knowing her time was limited, she was forced to choose one.

I wish I had time to go to the mall, but I'll put these hot pink Louboutin's on to distract him, she thought to herself. *Let me hurry up and finish my make up before my date comes. He asked me to have an open mind and I think that calls for a G-string...yaaaaaassss!* She giggled to herself.

Karrington walks in her bathroom and creates the perfect smoky eye and nude lip that she is known for. She looks down at her vibrating phone where a call was coming in. The caller ID read, **Daddy**.

She giggled and her heart beat a little faster because that is the name she gave Dom in her phone. *"Hello, Dominique,"* she said sweetly. *"I'm ready!"*

Dom, a stickler for punctuality, was relieved as he let her know he was pulling up outside her place. Karrington took one more look at herself before confidently strutting out of the house.

As she approached her front door, she could see Dom's frame through the glass. When she opened the door, they were both captivated by each other.

Karrington's dress perfectly hugged every curve of her body. Her brown hair fell just below her shoulders, and her lips were plump and soft. Dominique visually drank her in until her voice broke his concentration.

"Sir, are you going to say hello?"

He was so taken aback by her beauty he forgot to speak. The way she said "Sir" intrigued him. *"Yes, pardon me, Kid, hello,"* he said with a smile that made her feel special.

Continuing, he said *"I knew you would be beautiful. I just didn't know you would make me speechless."*

They both laughed and as she turned to lock her door, she felt his hand around her waist and she softly gasped. He kept his hands on her all the way to the car and Karrington thought nervously to herself, *he's already found my weak spot.*

Once they were seated in the car, they began talking about the coincidence of going to the same gym. Dom asked how the visit with her parents went, and they both disclosed that this was their first date in a long time.

"*Before I moved back to West Virginia, I went through a bad divorce,*" Karrington began. She stopped suddenly because she tends to overshare and she just didn't want this night to be affected by what she had left behind.

She finished with, "*I feel like this is a better move for me and I am much happier here.*"

Dominique noticed her pause, but he didn't push it. He didn't want this night to be tainted by anything. "*Well, change is good, Kid, and I'll be around. I'm here for as long as you need me.*" He punctuated that with a smile.

Karrington was thinking that she had just met him Friday, now she was in his car with him on Sunday, with with no clue where she was headed. "*Dominique?*" Karrington said softly.

"*Hmm?*" Dom glanced at her to let her know he was listening, before putting his eyes back on the road.

"*I was so looking forward to tonight that I forgot to ask you, where are we going? P.S. I also like the planning on your part and my favorite thing about this date is I didn't have to think about what I was going to wear.*"

"*We are going to the Aquarium Lounge. I closed off a section for us and I'll share more as the night goes on. Are you good with that answer?*"

Karrington didn't know how to preempt the evening. She kinda felt like she knew what was going on, but she kinda didn't. This was a new experience and she was gonna have to go with it, keeping an open mind like Dom requested.

They finally pulled up to the restaurant, and Dom drove to the valet station. As Karrington gathered her purse and throw, she glimpsed a black box with a red ribbon tied in a bow on the backseat. This piqued her curiosity but she just repeated Dom's request to herself. *Keep an open mind.*

The valet opened her door and Dom quickly made it to her side of the car. He saw her thigh as she swung her legs out of the car in what seemed like slow motion, and he couldn't help but stare.

He held his arm out, *"You ready, Kid?"* he asked.

She nodded, flashing him that smile. He says, *"I didn't tell you when I met you at your door, but you are really beautiful."*

She thanked him and she could see the black box in his hand. She tried to ignore the gift, but it was right there, so she had to ask. *"Dom, what's in the box?"*

He looked at her and pulled her in close and said, *"This box is for you and this dinner is for us. Tonight is your call. Tonight we are two individuals sharing a hedonistic evening, and we will decide after this evening how to go forward. But tonight, I'm yours and you're mine."*

Karrington was intoxicated by his words. As he pulled her closer, his lips barely grazed hers and he asked, *"Are you okay?"*

She didn't know what to say but she somehow remembered what she said earlier today. She looked up into his deep brown eyes and regained her positon on the ground. In a raspy and low voice, *"I'm all yours."*

They were escorted to their VIP area and once seated, Dominique could see the way Karrington's face was flushed and he leaned in and reassured her. *"I got you."*

Karrington looked at him with sincerity and said, *"I receive that."*

Dominique leaned in and softly kissed her on her cheek and called for the waiter so this night of adventure could begin.

Karrington was simultaneously comfortable and anxious. The night was young but she already knew with certainty that she had never experienced anything like this in her life. On the drive to dinner, she became amazed at how comfortable she was with Dominique, and all he had planned.

His selections for dinner were perfect. The champagne complemented the meal perfectly. The conversation was general, which helped her calm down from his introduction to the evening. Dominique wanted her close and then the next introduction to the night happened.

"Kid," he said. He clearly loved calling her that and she didn't mind. She actually thought it was cute, even in this passionate moment.

"I don't presume I know what you like, but I know what I like and I like you. I knew when I saw you enter the office building on your first day."

Karri turned her body to him to show him he had her full attention. *"I would like for you to share this night with me. Will you really have an open mind? I trust you and I hope you will trust me."*

She was quiet as he continued, *"Please open the box. It's for you and I would like for you to share this complete evening with me."*

Karri was all in and complied. She moved closer to him and placed her hand on the side of his face and said, *"You haven't given me a reason not to trust you Dom. I'm following your lead this evening."*

Her response made Dominique feel more at ease as he gave her the box. She took the box from his hands, untied the ribbon, and removed the top. Inside there was a black satin blindfold. She picked it up and he reached his hand out for her to give it to him.

Dominique instructed her to turn around and informed her about the rest of the evening. *"Kid, if you are not comfortable let me know and we can go in a different direction."*

Before she turned, she leaned in and kissed him and uttered what seemed to be her theme for the evening, *"I'm all yours."*

With that she turned around and he placed the blindfold on her face. After he secured it, his hands moved softly down her back until they were around her waist.

He could see her take a deep breath as he leaned in and said, *"There are going to be more moments like this. Come here."*

There was something about the way he said, *"Come here,"* that made her heed his command. Depending on only her senses and Dominique's voice, Karrington's body began to react to everything! His touch, his voice, his words, the unknown... she felt her body tingling in ways that it hadn't in a long time.

As they walked away from the table, he leaned into her and said, *"When I told you I trust you, I meant that. I'm going to take good care of you and all I want you to do is receive. Are you okay with that?"*

She turned her face in his direction and said, *"I trust you, Dom, and I'm enthused about this evening."* He kissed her on her forehead, put her in the car and pulled off.

As they drove, the fact that they were having a general conversation was not as odd, and it would seem to be. He was so respectful and made sure to give clear details.

"We're almost there and I really hope you enjoy this evening," he said in a gentle low voice. *"I really want you to enjoy yourself and your night with me."*

He spoke to her as if he was hoping she would still be interested, but her response was very reassuring. *"Dom, this night has been nothing I've experienced before. I'm anticipating every second."*

She couldn't see his smile, but she could hear it in voice with his response. *"Kid, it's about to get better."*

They turned a corner and she felt the car come to a stop. Dom opened her door, and reached down to help her out of the car., taking both her hands in his. When she was out of the car, he cupped her face gently and kissed her passionately.

Karrington could feel her whole body reacting to his kiss, as her senses were heightened. Dominique broke the kiss way too quickly for her liking and whispered, *"We are here and I'm here. I will be right here all night."*

They entered a building and Karrington's senses took over! She could feel Dom's hands around her waist. She heard Dom release a low sigh of pleasure. Intrigued, she held his hand a little tighter.

Karrington knew where she was, but she was a little nervous. She had never been to a Life Style club before, but what Dominique didn't know (yet), was that he was fulfilling one of her wildest fantasies.

She stopped walking, turned to him and asked, *"Dom, can you remove my blindfold please? I want to see you."*

Domonique was relieved and he obliged quickly. Once he removed the blindfold, he noticed Karrington's seductive eyes. She was focused on him. She leaned in and said, *"This is already the best night of my life. Thank you,"* and as she went on her toes, his lips met hers.

Dominique had secured a VIP room with champagne service. No words needed to be said. They understood everything each other had to say in that moment. They found themselves entangled in each other.

There was so much passion between them. Dominique softly touched her thigh and slowly moved his hand closer to her den of wetness. He was careful. He stopped at mid-thigh until she put her hands on top of his, instructing him to continue.

He felt the material of her g-string and said, *"I don't think you need these."*

"I don't either."

They continued to explore each other with their fingertips until Dom sensed that Karri was about to lose control. This is where he dominates.

"Kid, I am in control of your cums. They are mine and I want them when I want them...ok?"

Karrington found herself obeying him, as her heartbeat sped up. They finally pried themselves away from each other long enough to explore the club. There were rooms with just women, rooms with men and women and rooms that were available for others to watch.

Dominique let Karrington take the lead. He wanted her to be comfortable so he followed behind her. She stopped at a window where a threesome was taking place.

Karrington remained silent. Not taking her eyes off of the triple, she reached for his hands and guided them over her body. She put her hands on top of his, where her dress was gathered around her hips, and guided his fingers to her warm wetness. She looked at Dominique and let out a gasp as they slowly entered her.

"Are you ready?" He whispered.

She nodded.

Karrington is a very sexual being and being in this environment is what her dreams were made of. This had been a constant problem in her previous marriage. She had dreamed of moments like this. Now, tonight, being here with an almost stranger was a welcome stimulation for her body. As they re-entered their room, Dom asked whether she wanted the curtain opened or closed.

"Closed. Tonight I just want to be with you."

Dominique noted her implication that there was a possibility of them coming back. This took him over the edge.

"Karrington, let me know if there is something you want or don't, ok?"

With that he bent down and kissed her red lips. That was the first time she had heard him say her name and she was flushed from his tone. She'd never heard her name said like that before.

Everything seemed to go in slow motion. She could feel the strap of her dress fall but she never took their eyes off of Dom. She realized after a minute that she was wearing only heels, as Dom pulled away to sit down. As he stared at her she felt both power and anxiety. Neither said a word. His gaze was filled with admiration. She slowly let her walls fall and walked over to him.

Dominique was elated and in awe of Karrington. Her body was amazing. Sitting there, he watched her as she visibly relaxed in front of him. She touched her breasts, then slid her hands down her hips, eventually touching her wetness. He hadn't felt like the way he did in that moment in a very long time. He was mesmerized.

As she walked towards him, he couldn't wait to touch her. When his fingers found her skin, she moved his hands away. This turned him on more than she could ever know. Once she gave him permission to touch her, he picked her up so her wetness was on his eye level, and began to devour her with his tongue.

She eagerly responded to him. Her moans and movements caused him to lick her with more fervor, until she released her juices in his mouth. He slowly licked his way up her stomach until his eye met hers.

"Dom, I want you. I want to taste you."

He was pleased that she wanted to please him as he did her.

Karrington got on her knees. Her lips closed around his manhood and Dominique released a guttural moan that emboldened her. She slowly caressed his thighs with her hands while using her mouth to please him.

Karrington has never felt this free and that feeling caused her to vigorously suck Dominique, until she could feel herself cumming from giving him head. Dominique stopped her and helped her up.

Carrying her over to the large couch, he asked, *"Are you ready?"*

Karrington looked at him and said simply, *"Yes."*

As Dom entered Karrington, they locked eyes. The intensity was so high and their gasps were the only communication they used. They were focused on each other and the world around them seemed to melt away.

Dominique being a quick study, skillfully navigated her body. Her orgasms were coming. He was an excellent coach and his kink is pushing the limits, so her orgasms got him off. She screamed, *"Dominique I'm cumming!"*

Dominique said, *"I know you want to, but not yet."*

Karrington was spent and could hardly understand words. When Dominique told her she couldn't cum this made her body react in a way that she was unfamiliar with.

Dominique stood up and told her, *"I want to see you cum for me before I cum for you."*

Karrington's dreams were literally coming true by the second. Surprisingly, she found the words to say, *"Can you tell me what to do?"*

Her voice was innocent as if she's never masturbated before. Dominique was only too happy she asked because he likes to give directions.

"Open your legs so I can see you." Once she did that, he said, *"Good girl. Now suck on your finger to make it moist, and let me see you finger yourself until I tell you to stop."*

Karrington was just as turned on as Dominique. Her obedience was very erotic, and she could feel her wetness as she kept her eyes on him, while he watched her. *"Keep going. I want to see you make a mess for me. Such a good girl!"*

The more he talked she could feel her orgasm and she let him know. *"Dom, I'm cumming for you. I'm cumming for you!"*

"Open and let me see. Let me see you, baby girl. Let me see you make a mess for me." Dominique's voice was low and calm. He loved the look on Karrington's face. It made him want her even more.

"I'm cumming," she screamed again, as he quickly moved her fingers and entered her to feel her erupt on him.

"Yes, cum on me."

Karrington could feel her body tense, as Dominique eased inside her. She let out a pleasurable sound of relief on Dominique.

Dominique could feel her on him and he asked, *"Karrington, do you want me to cum for you now?"*

Karrington could barely speak, but she managed to get out a word, *"Please."*

Dominique continued to make slow, calculated strokes with his eyes on hers.

Karrington commanded in a low voice, *"Cum for me."*

That was just what he needed to hear. It had been a long time for Dominique, because he's a man of great restraint. He was content because he had been right about Karrington. All of those feelings, looking at her, and being inside of her brought on his release.

"I'm cumming for you," he asked where she wanted him to release it.

"Wherever you want, Dom," she purred.

He didn't want to move so he stayed inside as long as he could and he yelled out, *"I'm cumming!"*

They laid next to each other, completely satisfied and relieved, still not knowing where this would go after tonight. Dominique leaned back on his knees and watched as his pleasure flowed out of Karrington.

He dressed her silently, and kissed her gently. Then he said, *"I can't call you 'Kid' anymore. You are literally a good girl. You're my Good Girl."*

Karrington smiled, stepped into her stilettos and said, *"I'm fine with that, Dom. I'll be your Good Girl if you'll be my Guy."*

Dominique pulled her to him and said, *"You ready to go?"*

Karrington nodded yes and they walked out. He held her close on the walk to the car. When he put her in on her side, it was as if she fell into the seat.

He got in and looked over at her and said, *"I knew you were the one, I knew it."*

She smiled and asked, *"Dom, how do we do this, working together? I don't think I will ever forget this night."*

He looked over and said, *"We'll talk about what that looks like later. Let me get you home."*

The ride home was very different. They had a great conversation on the way back and learned a lot about each other. When they made it to Karrington's, he walked her to the door and kissed her good night.

"I'll see you in the morning, don't be late." She smiled and said, *"I won't Sir, I will be there bright and early."*

He walked her to the door and watched her get into her condo. As she locked her front door, she could hear his car speed off. She went into the bathroom and turned on the shower. She could still feel him inside of her. She could still feel her wetness.

As she showered the night away, she couldn't help but replay the entire night in her mind.

Karrington, this may be your best move yet, she thought as she got in bed. After she got in bed, she only had seconds before she fell asleep and she couldn't wait till morning to see her Guy again.

Are there any roses
without a thorn ?

It's ya girl Millichun!!!
Follow me to find out

@millichun | @millichun08